Councillor Krespel

E.T.A. Hoffmann

ISBN-13: 978-1537604640

The man whom I am going to tell you about was Krespel, a Member of Council in the town of H____. This Krespel was the most extraordinary character that I have ever come across in all my life. When I first arrived in H____ whole town was talking of him, because one of his most extraordinary pranks chanced to be in full swing. He was a very clever lawyer and diplomat, and a certain German prince—not a person of great importance—had employed him to draw up a memorial, concerning claims of his on the Imperial Chancery, which had been eminently successful. As Krespel had often said he never could meet with a house quite to his mind, this prince, as recompense for his services, undertook to pay for the building of one, to be planned by Krespel according to the dictates of his fancy. He also offered to buy a site for it; but Krespel determined to build it in a delightful piece of garden ground of his own, just outside the town-gate. So he got together all the necessary building materials, and had them laid down in this piece of ground. After which, he was to be seen all day long, in his usual extraordinary costume—which he always made with his own hands, on peculiar principles of his own—slaking the lime, sifting the gravel, arranging the stones in heaps, etc., etc. He had not gone to any architect for a plan. But one fine day he walked in upon the principal builder, and told him to come next morning to his garden, with the necessary workmen—stonemasons, hodmen and so forth—and build him a house. The builder, of course, asked to see the plan, and was not a little astonished when Krespel said there was no plan and no occasion for one; everything would go on all right without one.

The builder arrived next morning with his men, and found a great rectangular trench, carefully dug in the ground. 'This is the foundation,' Krespel said. 'So set to work, and go on building the walls till I tell you to stop.'

'But what about the doors and windows?' asked the builder. 'Are there to be no partition walls?'

'Just you do as I tell you, my good man ' said Krespel as calmly as possible come quite right in its own good time.'

Nothing but the prospect of liberal payment induced the man to have anything to do with so preposterous a job—but never was there a piece of work carried through so merrily; for it was amid the ceaseless jokes and laughter of the workmen—who never left the ground, where abundance of victuals and drink was always at hand—that the four walls rose with incredible speed, till one day Krespel cried 'Stop!'

Mallets and chisels paused. The men came down from their scaffolds and formed a circle about Krespel, each grinning countenance seeming to say—'What's going to happen now?'

'Out of the way!' cried Krespel, who hastened to one end of the garden, and then paced slowly towards his rectangle of stone walls. On reaching the side of it which was nearest—the one, that is, towards which he had been marching—he shook his head dissatisfied, went to the other end of the garden, then paced up to the wall as before, shaking his head, dissatisfied, once more.

This process he repeated two or three times; but at last, going straight up to the wall till he touched it with the point of his nose, he cried out, loud: 'Come here, you fellows, come here! Knock me in the door! Knock me in a door here!' He gave the size it was to be, accurately in feet and inches; and what he told them to do they did. When the door was knocked through, he walked into the house, and smiled pleasantly at the builder's remark that the walls were just the proper height for a nice two-storied house. He walked meditatively up and down inside, the masons following him with their tools, and whenever he cried 'here a window six feet by four; a little one yonder three feet by two,' out flew the stones as directed.

It was during these operations that I arrived in H____ , and it was entertaining in the extreme to see some hundreds of people collected outside the garden, all hurrahing whenever the stones flew out, and a window appeared where none had been expected. The house was all finished in the same fashion, everything being done according to Krespel's directions as given on the spot. The quaintness of the proceeding, the irresistible feeling that it was all going to turn out so marvelously better than was to have been expected; but, particularly Krespel's liberality, which, by the way, cost him nothing, kept everybody in the best of humor. So the difficulties attending this remarkable style of house-building were got over, and in a very brief time there stood a fully-finished house, which had the maddest appearance certainly, from the outside, no two windows being alike and so forth, but was a marvel of comfort and convenience within. Everybody said so who entered it, and I was of the same opinion, when Krespel admitted me to it after I made his acquaintance.

It was some time, however, ere I did so. He had been so engrossed by his building operations that he had never gone, as he did at other times, to lunch at Professor M 's on Thursdays, saying he should not cross his threshold till after his house-warming. His friends were expecting a grand entertainment on that occasion. However, he invited nobody but the workmen who built the house. Them he entertained with the most recherché dishes. Journeymen masons feasted on venison pasties; carpenters' apprentices and hungry hodmen for once in their lives stayed their appetites with roast pheasant and pate de foie ares. In the evening their wives and daughters came, and there was a fine ball. Krespel just waltzed a little with the foremen's wives, and then sat down with the town-band, took a fiddle, and led the dance-music till daylight.

On the Thursday after this house-warming, which had established Krespel in the position of a popular character—'a friend to the working classes' at last met him at Professor M 's, to my no small gratification. The most extravagant imagination could not invent anything more extraordinary than Krespel's style of behavior. His movements were awkward, abrupt, constrained, so that you expected him to bump against the furniture and knock things over' or do some mischief or other every moment. But he never did; and you soon noticed that the lady of the house never changed color ever so little, although he went floundering heavily and uncertainly about, close to tables covered with valuable china, or maneuvering in dangerous proximity to a great mirror reaching from floor to ceiling; even when he took up a valuable china jar, painted with flowers, and whirled it about near the window to admire the play of the light on its colors. In fact, whilst we were waiting for luncheon, he inspected and scrutinized everything in the room with the utmost minuteness, even getting up upon a cushioned arm-chair to take a picture down from the wall and hang it up again.

All this time he talked a great deal; often (and this was more noticeable while we were at luncheon) darting rapidly from one subject to another, and at other times—unable to get away from some particular idea—he would keep beginning at it again and again, and get into labyrinths of confusion over it, till something else came into his head. Sometimes the tone of his voice was harsh and strident, at other times it would be soft and melodious; but it was always completely inappropriate to what he happened to be talking about. For instance, as we were discussing music, and some one was praising a new composer, Krespel smiled, and said in his gentle cantabile tone, 'I wish to heaven the devil would hurl the wretched music-perverter ten thousand millions of fathoms deep into the abysses of hell!' after which he screamed out violently and wildly, 'She's an angel of heaven, all compounded of the purest, divines" music': and the tears came to his eyes. It was some time ere we remembered that, about an hour before, we had been talking of a particular prima donna.

There was a hare at table, and I noticed that he carefully polished the bones on his plate, and made particular inquiries for the feet, which were brought to him, with many smiles, by the professor's little daughter of fifteen. All through luncheon the children had kept their eyes upon him as on a favorite, and now they came up to him, though they kept a respectful distance of two or three paces. 'What's going to happen?' thought I. The dessert came, and Krespel took a small box from his pocket, out of which he brought a miniature turning-lathe, made of steel, which he screwed on to the table, and proceeded to turn, from the bones, with wonderful skill and rapidity, all sorts of charming little boxes, balls, etc., which the children took possession of with cries of delight.

As we rose from table, the professor's niece said: 'And how is our dear Antonia, Mr. Krespel?'

'Our—OUR dear Antonia!' he answered, in his sustained singing tone, most unpleasant to hear. At first he made the sort of face which a person makes who bites into a bitter orange and wants to look as if it were a sweet one; but soon this face changed to a perfectly terrible-looking mask, out of which grinned a bitter, fierce—nay' as it seemed to me, altogether diabolical, sneer of angry scorn.

The professor hastened up to him. In the look of angry reproach which he cast at his niece I read that she had touched some string which jarred most discordantly within Krespel.

'How are things going with the violins?' asked the professor, taking Krespel by both hands.

The cloud cleared away from his face, and he answered in his harsh rugged tone, 'Splendidly, Professor. You remember my telling you about a magnificent Amati, which I got hold of by a lucky accident a short time ago? I cut it open this very morning, and expect that Antonia has finished taking it to pieces by this time.'

'Antonia is a dear, good child,' said the Professor.

'Ay! that she is—that she is!' screamed Krespel and, seizing his hat and stick, was off out of the house like a flash of lightning.

As soon as he was gone, I eagerly begged the Professor to tell me all about those violins, and more especially about Antonia.

'Ah,' said the Professor, 'Krespel is an extraordinary man; he studies fiddle-making in a peculiar fashion of his own.'

'Fiddle-making?' cried I in amazement.

'Yes,' said the Professor; 'connoisseurs consider that Krespel's violin-making is unrivalled at the present day. Formerly, when he turned out any special chef-d'oeuvre, he would allow other people to play upon it; but now he lets no one touch them but himself. When he has finished a fiddle, he plays upon it for an hour or two (he plays magnificently, with a power, a feeling and expression which the greatest professional violinists rarely equal, let alone surpass). Then he hangs it up on the wall beside the others, and never touches it again, nor lets anyone else lay hands upon it.'

'And Antonia?' I eagerly asked.

'Well, that,' said the Professor, 'is an affair which would give me a very shady opinion of Krespel, if I didn't know what a thoroughly good fellow he is; so that I feel convinced there is some mystery about it which we don't at present fathom. When he first came here, some years ago, he lived like a hermit, with an old housekeeper, in a gloomy house in Street. His eccentricities soon attracted people's attention, but when he saw this, he quickly sought and made acquaintances. Just as was the case in my house, people got so accustomed to him that they couldn't get on without him. In spite of his rough exterior even the children got fond of him, though they were never troublesome to him, but always looked upon him with a certain amount of awe which prevented over-familiarity. You have seen how he attracts children by all sorts of ingenious tricks. Everybody looked upon him as a regular old bachelor and woman-hater, and he gave no sign to the contrary; but after he had been here some time, he went off on some excursion or other, no one knew where, and it was some months before he came back.

'The second evening after his return, his windows were lighted up in an unusual way—and that was enough to attract the neighbors' attention. Presently, a most extraordinarily beautiful female voice was heard singing to a pianoforte accompaniment. Soon the tones of a violin were heard joining in, responding to the voice in brilliant, fiery emulation. It was easy to distinguish that it was Krespel who was playing. I joined the little crowd assembled outside the house myself, to listen to the wonderful concert, and I can assure you that the greatest prima donnas I have ever heard were poor everyday performers compared to the lady we heard that night. I had never before had any conception of such long-sustained notes, such nightingale roulades, such crescendoes and diminuendoes, such swellings to an organ-like forte, such dyings down to the most imperceptible whisper. There was not a soul in all the crowd able to resist the magic spell of that wonderful singing; and when she stopped, you heard nothing but sighs breaking the silence. It was probably about midnight, when all at once we heard Krespel talking loudly and excitedly; another male voice, to judge by the tone of it, bitterly reproaching him about something, and a woman intervening as best she could—tearfully, in broken phrases. Krespel screamed louder and louder, till at last he broke into that horrible singing tone which you know. A loud shriek from the lady interrupted him: then all was as still as death; and suddenly steps came rapidly down the stairs, and a young man came out, sobbing, and, jumping into a carriage which was standing near, drove rapidly away.

'The next day Krespel appeared quite in his ordinary condition, as if nothing had happened, and no one had the courage to allude to the events of the previous night; but the housekeeper said Krespel had brought home a most beautiful lady, quite young; that he called her Antonia, that it was she who had sung so splendidly; and that a young gentleman had also come, who seemed to be deeply attached to Antonia, and, as she supposed, was engaged to her; but that he had had to go away, for Krespel had insisted on it.

'What Antonia's precise position with respect to Krespel is, remains a mystery; at all events he treats her in the most tyrannical style. He watches her as a cat does a mouse, or as Dr. Bartolo, in *Il Barbiere*, does his niece. She scarcely dares to look out of the window. On the rare occasions when he can be prevailed upon to take her into society, he watches her with Argus-eyes, and won't suffer a note of music to be heard, far less that she shall sing; neither will he now allow her to sing in his own house; so that, since that celebrated night, Antonia's singing has become, for the people of the town, a sort of romantic legend, as of some splendid miracle; and even those who never heard her often say, when some celebrated prima donna comes to sing at a concert, "Good gracious! what a wretched caterwauling all this is. Nobody can sing but Antonia!"'

You know how anything of this sort always fascinates me, and you can imagine how essential it became to me that I should make Antonia's acquaintance. I had often heard popular references to the famous Antonia's singing, but I had had no idea that this glorious creature was there, on the spot, held in thralldom by the crack-brained Krespel, as by some tyrant enchanter. Naturally, that night in my dreams I heard Antonia singing in the most magnificent style; and as she was imploring me, in the most moving manner, to set her free, in a gloriously lovely adagio—absurdly enough, it seemed as if I had composed it myself—I at once made up my mind that, by some means or other, I would make my way into Krespel's house and, like another Astolfo, set this Queen of Song free from her shameful bonds.

Things came about, however, in a way that I had not anticipated; for after I had once or twice met Krespel and had a talk with him about fiddle-making, he asked me to go and see him. I went, and he showed me his violin treasures: there were some thirty of them hanging in a cabinet; and there was one, remarkable above the rest, with all the marks of the highest antiquity (a carved lion's head at the end of the tail-piece, etc.), which was hung higher than the others, with a wreath of flowers on it, and which seemed to reign over the rest as queen.

'That violin,' said Krespel, when I questioned him about it, 'is very remarkable and the unique creation of some ancient master, most probably about the time of Tartini. I am quite convinced there is something most peculiar about its interior construction, and that, if I were to take it to pieces, I should discover a certain secret which I have long been in search of. But—you may laugh at me if you like—that lifeless thing, which I myself inspire with life and language, often speaks to me, out of itself, in an extraordinary manner; and when I first played upon it, I felt as if I were merely the magnetiser—the mesmerist—who acts upon his subject in such sort that she relates in words what she is seeing with her inward vision. No doubt you think me an ass to have any faith in nonsense of this sort; still, it is the fact that I have never been able to prevail upon myself to take that lifeless thing there to pieces. I am glad I never did, for since Antonia has been here, I now and then play to her on that fiddle; she is fond of hearing it—very fond.'

He exhibited so much emotion as he said this, that I was emboldened to say 'Ah! dear Mr. Krespel, won't you be so kind as to let me hear you play on it?'

But he made one of his bitter-sweet faces, and answered in his cantabile sostenuto: 'No, no, my dear young man, that would ruin everything;' and I had to go and admire a number of curiosities, principally childish trash, till at length he dived into a chest and brought out a folded paper, which he put into my hand with much solemnity, saying: 'There' you are very fond of music: accept tints as a present from me, and always prize it beyond everything. It is a souvenir of great value.' With which he took me by my shoulders and gently shoves me out of the door, with an embrace on the threshold—in short, he symbolically kicked me out of his house.

When I opened the paper which he had given me, I found a small piece of the first string of a violin, about an eighth of an inch in length, and on the paper was written—'Portion of the first string of Seamitz's violin on which he played his last Concerto.'

The calmly insulting style in which I had been shown to the door the moment I had said a word about Antonia, seemed to indicate that I should probably never be allowed to see her; however, the second time I went to Krespel's I found her there in his room, helping him to put a fiddle together. Her exterior did not strike me much at first, but after a short time one could not resist the charm of her lovely blue Byes, rosy lips, and exquisitely expressive, tender face. She was very pale; but when anyone said anything interesting, a bright color and a very sweet smile appeared in her face; but the color quickly died down to a pale-rose tint. She and I talked quite unconstrainedly and pleasantly together, and I saw none of those Argus-glances which the Professor had spoken about. Krespel pursued his ordinary, beaten track, and seemed rather to approve of my being friendly with Antonia than otherwise. Thus it came about that I went there pretty often, and our little group of three got so accustomed to each other's society that we much enjoyed ourselves in our quiet way. Krespel was always entertaining with his strange eccentricities; but it was really Antonia who drew me to the house, and made me put up with a great deal which, impatient as I was in those days, I should never have endured but for her. In Krespel's quirks and cranks there was often a good deal which was tedious, and not in the best of taste. What most annoyed me was that, whenever I led the conversation to music—particularly to vocal music —he would burst in, in that horrible singing voice of his, and smiling like a demon, with something wholly irrelevant, and generally absolutely unimportant at the same time. From Antonia's looks of annoyance on those occasions, it was clear that he did this merely to prevent me from asking her to sing. However, I wasn't going to give in: the more he objected, the more determined was I to carry my point I felt that I must hear her, or die of my dreams of it.

There came an evening when Krespel was in particularly good humor. He had taken an old Cremona violin to pieces, and found that the sound-post of it was about half a line more perpendicular than usual. An important detail!—of priceless practical value! I was fortunate enough to start him off on the true style of violin playing. The style of the great old masters—copied by them from that of the really grand singers—of which he spoke, led to the observation that now the direct converse held good, and that singers copied the scale, and the skipping 'passages' of the instrumentalists. 'What,' said I, hastening to the piano and sitting down at it, 'can be more preposterous than such disgusting mannerisms, more like the noise of peas rattling on the floor of a barn than music?' I went on to sing a number of those modern cadenza-passages, which go yooping up and down the scale, more like a child's humming-top than anything else, and I struck a feeble chord or two by way of accompaniment. Krespel laughed immoderately, and cried 'Ha! ha! ha! I could fancy I was listening to some of our German Italians, or our Italian Germans, pumping out some aria of Pucitta or Portugallo, or some other such maestro di capella, or rather schiavo d'un primo uomo.'

'Now,' thought I, 'is my chance at last.—I am sure Antonia,' I said, turning to her, 'knows nothing of all that quavering stuff,' and I commenced to roll out a glorious soulful aria of old Leonardo Leo's.

Antonia's cheeks glowed; a heavenly radiance beamed from her beautiful eyes; she sprang to the piano; she opened her lips—but Krespel instantly made a rush at her; shoved her out of the room and, seizing me by the shoulders, shrieked—'My boy, my boy, my boy!'

Then taking me by the hand and bowing his head most courteously he continued, in a soft and gentle singing voice, 'No doubt, my dear young man, it would be an unpardonable breach of courtesy and politeness if I were to proceed to express, in plain and unmistakable terms, and wide all the energy at my command, my desire that the devil of hell himself might crutch hold of that throat of yours, here on the spot, with his red-hot talons. Leaving that on one side for the moment, however, you will admit, my very dear young friend, that it's getting pretty late in the evening, and will soon be dark; and as there are no lamps lighted, even if I were not to pitch you down stairs, you might run a certain risk of damaging your precious limbs. So go away home, like a nice young gentleman, and don't forget your good friend Krespel, if you should never—never, you understand—find him at home again when you happen to call.' With which he took me in his arms, and slowly worked his way with me to the door in such fashion that I could not manage to set eyes on Antonia again, even for a moment.

You will admit that, situated as I was, it was impossible for me to give him a good hiding, as probably I ought to have done by rights. The Professor laughed tremendously, and declared that I had seen the last of Krespel for good and all; and Antonia was too precious, I might say too sacred, in my sight for me to go playing the languishing amoroso under her window. I left her, broken-hearted; but, as is the case with matters of the kind, the bright tints of the picture in my fancy gradually faded and toned down with the lapse of time; and Antonia, ay, even Antonia's singing, which I had never heard, came to shine upon my memory only like some beautiful, far-away vision, bathed in rosy radiance.

Two years afterwards when I was settled in B , I had occasion to make a journey into the South of Germany. One evening I saw the familiar towers of H rising into sight against the dewy, roseate evening sky; and as I came nearer, a strange, indescribable feeling of anxiety and alarm took possession of me, lying on my heart like a weight of lead. I could scarcely breathe. I got out of the carriage into the open air. The oppression amounted to actual physical pain. Presently I thought I could hear the notes of a solemn hymn floating on the air; it grew more distinct, and I made out male voices singing a chorale.

'What's this, what's this?' I cried as it pierced through my heart like a dagger stab.

'Don't you see, sir?' said the postilion, walking beside me, 'it's a funeral going on in the churchyard.'

We were, in fact, close to the cemetery, and I saw a circle of people in black assembled by a grave, which was being filled in. The tears came to my eyes. I felt as if somehow all the happiness and joy of my life were being buried in that grave. I had been descending the hill pretty quickly so that I could not now see into the cemetery. The chorale ceased, and I saw, near the gate, men in black coming away from the funeral. The Professor with his niece on his arm, both in deep mourning, passed close to me without noticing me. The niece had her handkerchief to her eyes and was sobbing bitterly.

I felt I could not go into the town; so I sent my servant with the carriage to the usual hotel, and walked out into the well known country to try if I could shake off the strange condition I was in, which I ascribed to physical causes, being overheated and tired with my journey, etc. When I reached the alley which leads to the public gardens, I saw a most extraordinary sight— Krespel, led along by two men in deep mourning, whom he seemed to be trying to escape from by all sorts of extraordinary leaps and bounds. He was dressed as usual, in his wonderful grey coat of his own making; but from his little three-cornered hat, which he had cocked over one ear in a martial manner, hung a very long, narrow streamer of black crepe, which fluttered playfully in the breeze. Round his waist he had buckled a black sword-belt, but instead of a sword he had stuck a long fiddle bow into it. The blood ran cold in my veins. 'He has gone quite mad,' I said as I followed them slowly.

They took him to his own door, where he embraced them, laughing loudly. When they left him, he noticed me, and after staring at me in silence for a considerable time, said in a mournful, hollow voice: 'Glad to see you, young fellow. You know all about it.' He seized me by the arm, dragged me into the house, and upstairs to the room where the violins hung. They were all covered with crepe, but the masterpiece by the unknown maker was not in its place; a wreath of cypress hung in its stead.

I knew then what had happened. 'Antonia, alas! Antonia,' I cried in uncontrollable anguish.

Krespel was standing in front of me with his arms folded, like a man turned to stone.

'When she died,' he said, very solemnly, 'the soundpost of that fiddle broke with a shivering crash. The faithful thing could only live with her and in her; it is lying with her in her grave.' I sank overwhelmed into a chair; but Krespel began singing a merry ditty, in a hoarse voice; and it was a truly awful sight to see him dancing, as he sang it, upon one foot, while the crepe on his hat kept flapping about the fiddles on the wall; and I could not help giving a scream of horror as, during one of his rapid gyrations, this crepe streamer came wafting over my face, for I felt as if the touch of it must infallibly infect me, and drag me, too, down into the black, terrible abyss of madness.

At this Krespel suddenly stopped dancing, and said in his singing voice: 'What did you shriek out like that for, my boy? Did you see the angel of death? It's generally before the funeral that people see him!' Then, walking into the middle of the floor, he drew the bow out of his belt and, raising it with both hands above his head, he broke it into splinters. Whereupon he laughed long and loud, and cried, 'The staff's broken over me now, you think, my boy, don't you? nothing of the kind, nothing of the kind!

I'm free now—I'm free! I'm free! And fiddles I'll make no more, boys! And fiddles I'll make no more! Hurray! hurray! hip-hip hurray! Oh! fiddles I'll make no more.'

This he sang to a hideously merry tune, dancing about on one foot again as he did so.

Horrified, I was making for the door; but he held me back, saying quite quietly and soberly this time: 'Don't go away, my dear young fellow, and don't imagine that these outbreaks mean that I'm mad. But my grief is so terrible that I can scarcely bear it any longer. No, no, I am as sane as you are, and as much in my senses. The trouble is, a little while ago I made myself a nightshirt, and thought when I had it on I should look like Destiny, or God.'

He went on spouting the wildest incoherences for a time, till he sank down, completely exhausted. The old housekeeper came at my summons, and I was thankful when I found myself outside in the open air.

I never doubted for an instant that Krespel had gone completely mad; but the Professor maintained the contrary. 'There are certain people,' he said, 'whom Nature, or some malign destiny, has deprived of the cover—the exterior envelope—under which we others carry on our madnesses unseen. They are like certain insects who have transparent integuments, which—since we see the play of their muscular movements—give the effect of a malformation. But actually they are perfectly normal. What never passes beyond the sphere of thought in us becomes action in Krespel. The bitter scorn and rage which the soul, imprisoned as it is in earthly conditions of being and action, often vividly feels, Krespel expresses in his external life, by extraordinary gesticulations and frantic movements. But those are his lightning conductors. What comes out of the earth he delivers back to the earth again; the heavenly he retains, and consequently apprehends it quite clearly and distinctly with his inner consciousness, notwithstanding all the crankiness which we see sparking out of him. No doubt Antonia's unexpected loss touches him very keenly, but I bet you that he'll be going on at his usual jog trot tomorrow, as if nothing had happened.'

And it turned out very much as the Professor had expected: Krespel appeared next morning very much as if nothing had happened. Only he announced that he had given up fiddle-making, and would never play on a fiddle again. And, it afterwards appeared, he kept his word.

All that I had heard from the Professor strengthened my conviction that the relation in which Antonia had stood to Krespel so very intimate, and so carefully kept unexplained—as also the fact that she was dead, most probably involved him in a situation of some gravity, from which it might be no easy matter for him to escape. I made up my mind that I would not leave H until I had given him the full benefit of my ideas on this subject. My notion was to thoroughly alarm him, to appeal to his conscience and, if I could, constrain him to a full confession of his crime. The more I considered the matter the clearer it seemed that he must be a terrible villain; and all the more eloquent and impressive grew the allocution which I mentally got ready to deliver to him, and which gradually took the form of a regular masterpiece of rhetoric.

Thus prepared for my attack, I betook myself to him one morning in a condition of much virtuous indignation. I found him making children's toys at his turning lathe, with a tranquil smile on his face.

'How,' said I, 'is it possible that your conscience can allow you to be at peace for an instant, when the thought of the horrible crime you have been guilty of must perpetually sting you like a serpent's tooth?'

He laid down his tools, and stared at me in astonishment. 'What do you mean, my good sir?' he said. 'Sit down on that chair there.'

But I continued with much warmth, and distinctly accused him of having caused Antonia's death, threatening him with the vengeance of Heaven. Nay more, being full of juridical zeal—as I had just been inducted into a judicial appointment—I went on to assure him that I should consider it my duty to leave no stone unturned to bring the affair thoroughly to light, so as to deliver him into the hands of earthly justice. I was a little put out, I admit, when on the conclusion of my rather pompous harangue, Krespel merely looked at me, without a word in reply, as if waiting for what I had to say next; and I tried to find something further to add: but everything that occurred to me seemed so silly and feeble that I held my peace. He seemed rather to enjoy this breakdown in my eloquence, and a bitter smile passed over his face.

But then he became very grave, and said in a solemn tone: 'My good young sir! Very likely you think me a fool—or a madman. I forgive you. We are both in the same madhouse, and you object to my thinking myself God the Father, because you think you are God the Son. How do you suppose you can enter into another person's life, utterly unknown to you in all its complicated turnings and windings, and pick up and follow all its deeply hidden threads? She is gone, and the mystery is solved!'

He stopped, rose and walked two or three times up and down the room. I ventured to ask for some explanation. He looked at me fixedly, took me by the hand, and led me to the french window, opening both panes. Then, leaning upon the sill with both his arms, and looking out into the garden, he told me the story of his life. When he had ended I left him, deeply affected and bitterly ashamed.

Antonia's history was roughly as follows:

Some twenty years previously, his fancy for making a collection of the finest violins of the great old makers had taken him to Italy. At that time he had not begun to make violins himself nor, consequently, to take them to pieces. At Venice he heard the renowned prima donna, Angela—at that time starring in the leading roles at the Teatro di San Benedetto. She was as unique in her beauty as in her art: and well became, and deserved, her name of Angela. He sought her acquaintance and, in spite of all his rugged uncouthness, his most remarkable violin playing, with its combination of great originality, force and tenderness, speedily won her artist's heart.

A close intimacy led, in a few weeks, to a marriage—which was not made public because Angela would neither leave the stage, give up her well-known name, nor tack on to it the strangely-sounding 'Krespel.'

He described, with the bitterest irony, the quite peculiar ingenuity with which Signora Angela began, as soon as she was his wife, to torment and torture him. All the selfishness, caprice, and obstinacy of all the prima donnas on earth rolled into one were, so Krespel considered, incorporated in Angela's little body. Whenever he tried to assert his true position in the smallest degree, she would launch a swarm of abbates, maestros, and academicos about his ears who, not knowing his real relations with her, would snub him, and set him down as a wretched, unendurable ass of an amateur inamorato, incapable of adapting himself to the Signora's charming and interesting humors.

After one of those stormy scenes, Krespel had flown off to Angela's country house, and improvising on his Cremona, was forgetting the sorrows of the day. He had not been playing long, however, when the Signora, who had followed him, came into the room. She happened to be in a tender mood: she embraced Krespel with sweet, languishing glances; she laid her little head upon his shoulder. But Krespel, lost in the world of his harmonies, went on fiddling, so that the walls re-echoed; and it so chanced that he touched the Signora, a trifle ungently, with his bow arm. Blazing up like a fury, she screamed out, 'Bestia tedesca,' snatched the violin out of his hand, and dashed it to pieces on a marble table. Krespel stood before her for a moment, a statue of amazement, and then, as if awaking from a dream, he grasped the Signora with his giant's strength, pitched her out of the window of her own palazzo, and set off — without concerning himself further about the matter—to Venice, and thence to Germany.

It was some little time before he quite realized what he had done. Though he knew the window was only some five feet from the ground, and the necessity of throwing the Signora out of it under the circumstances was quite indisputable, still he felt very anxious as to the results, inasmuch as she had given him to understand that he was about to be a father.

He was almost afraid to make any inquiries, and was not a little surprised, some eight months afterwards, to receive an affectionate letter from his beloved wife, in which she did not say a syllable about the little circumstance which had occurred at the country palazzo, but announced that she was the happy mother of a charming little daughter, and prayed the 'marito amato e pane felicissimo' to come as quickly as he could to Venice. However Krespel didn't go, but made inquiries as to the state of affairs through a trusted friend. He was told that the Signora had dropped down on to the grass as lightly as a bird, and the only results of her fall were mental ones. She had been like a new creature after Krespel's heroic achievement. All her willfulness and charming caprices had disappeared completely; and the maestro who wrote the music for the next Carnival considered himself the luckiest man under the sun; inasmuch as the Signora sang all his arias without one of the thousand alterations which, in ordinary circumstances, she would have insisted on his making in them. Krespel's friend added that it was most desirable to give no publicity to what had occurred; because, otherwise, prima donnas would be getting pitched out of windows every day.

Krespel was in great excitement. He ordered horses. He got into the post-chaise.

'Stop a moment, though,' he said. 'Isn't it a positive certainty that, as soon as I make my appearance, the evil spirit will take possession of Angela again? I've thrown her out of window once already. What should I do a second time? What is there left to do?'

So he got out of the carriage, wrote an affectionate letter to his wife, and—remained in Germany. They carried on a warm correspondence. Assurances of affection, fond imaginings, regrets for the absence of the beloved, etc., etc., flew backwards and forwards between H and Venice. Angela came to Germany, as we know, and shone as prima donna on the boards at F____. Though she was no longer young, she carried everything before her by the irresistible charm of her singing. Her voice had lost nothing at that time. Meanwhile Antonia had grown up; and her mother could scarce find words in which to describe to Krespel, how a Cantatrice of the first rank was blossoming forth in Antonia. Krespel's friends in F____, too, kept on telling him of this; begging him to go there and hear these two remarkable singers. Of course they had no idea of the relationship in which Krespel stood to them. He would fain have gone and seen his daughter, whom he treasured in the depths of his heart, and whom he often saw in dreams. But whenever he thought of his wife his spirits sank: and so he stayed at home, amongst his dismembered fiddles.

I daresay you remember a very promising young composer in F____ of the name of B____, who suddenly ceased to be heard of— no one knew why: perhaps you may have known him. Well, he fell deeply in love with Antonia; she returned his affection, and he urged her mother to consent to a union consecrated by art. Angela was quite willing, and Krespel gave his consent all the more readily because this young maestro's writings had found favor before his critical judgment. Krespel was expecting to hear of the marriage every day, when there came a letter with a black seal, addressed in a stranger's hand. A certain Dr. M____ wrote to say that Angela had been taken seriously ill, in consequence of a chill caught at the theatre, and had passed away on the very night before the day fixed for Antonia's marriage. He added that Angela had told him she was Krespel's wife, and Antonia his daughter; so that he ought to come and take charge of her.

Deeply as he was shocked by Angela's death, he could not but feel that a certain disturbing element was removes from his life, and that he could breathe freely for the first time for many a long day. You cannot imagine how affectingly he described the moment when he saw Antonia for the first time. In the very oddness of his description of it lay a wonderful power of expression which I am unable to give any idea of. Antonia had all the charm and attractiveness of Angela, with none of her nasty thorny side. There was no cloven hoof peeping out anywhere. B____ , her husband that was to have been, came. With delicate insight, Antonia saw into the depths of her strange father's mind, and understood him. So she sang one of those motets of Old Padre Martini which she knew Angela used to sing to him in the heyday of their love. He shed rivers of tears. Never had he heard even Angela sing so splendidly. The tone of Antonia's voice was quite sui generis— at times it was like the Aeolian harp, at others like the trilling roulades of the nightingale. It seemed as though there could not be space for those chords in a human breast. Glowing with love and happiness, Antonia sang all her loveliest songs, and B____ played between whiles as only ecstatic inspiration can play. At first Krespel swam in ecstasy. Then he grew thoughtful and silent, and finally sprang up, pressed Antonia to his heart, and said, gently and imploringly, 'Don't sing any more, if you love me. It breaks my heart. The fear of it—the fear of it! Don't sing any more.'

'No,' said Krespel next morning to Dr. M____ , 'when, during her singing, her color contracted to two dark red spots on her white cheeks, it was no longer a mere everyday family likeness—it was what I had been dreading.'

The doctor, whose face at the beginning of the conversation had expressed deep anxiety, said: 'Perhaps it may be that she has exerted herself too much in singing when over-young, or her inherited temperament may be the cause. But Antonia has an organic disease of the chest. It is that which gives her voice its extraordinary power, and its most remarkable timbre, which is almost beyond the scope of the ordinary human voice. At the same time it spells her early death. If she goes on singing, six months is the utmost I can promise her.'

This pierced Krespel's heart with a thousand daggers. It was as if some beautiful tree had suddenly come into his life, all covered with peerless blossoms, and was now sawn across at the root. His decision was made at once. He told Antonia all. He left it to her to decide whether she would follow her lover, yield to his and the world's claims on her, and die young; or bestow upon her father, in his declining years, a peace and happiness such as he had never known, and live many a year in so doing.

She fell sobbing into her father's arms. It was beyond his power to think at such a moment. He felt too keenly all the anguish involved in either alternative. He discussed the matter with B____ ; but although her lover asseverated that Antonia should never sing a single note, Krespel knew too well that he never would be able to resist the temptation to hear her sing—compositions of his own at all events. Then the world—the musical public—though it knew the true state of the case, would never give up its claims upon her. The musical public is a cruel race; selfish and terrible where its own enjoyment is in question.

Krespel disappeared with Antonia from F , and came to H____. B____ heard with despair of their departure, followed on their track, and arrived at H____ at the same time as they did.

'Only let me see him once, and then die!' Antonia implored.

'Die—die!' cried Krespel in the wildest fury.

His daughter, the only creature in the wide world who could fire him with a bliss he had never otherwise felt, the only being who had ever made life endurable to him, was tearing herself violently away from him. So the worst might happen, and he would give no sign.

B____ sat down to the piano, Antonia sang, and Krespel played the violin, till suddenly the dark red spots came to Antonia's cheeks. Then Krespel ordered a halt, but when B____ took his farewell she fell down insensible in a swoon.

'I thought she was dead,' Krespel said, 'for I quite expected it would kill her; and as I had wound myself up to expect the worst, I kept quite calm and self-possessed. I took hold of B____ by the shoulders (in his frightful consternation he was staring before him like a sheep), and said (here he fell into his singing voice), "My dear Mr. Pianoforte teacher, now that you have killed the woman you were going to marry by your own deliberate act, perhaps you will be so kind as to take yourself off out of this with as little trouble as you can, unless you choose to stay till I run this little hunting knife through you, so that my daughter, who, as you see, is looking rather white, may derive a shade or two of color from that precious blood of yours. Even though you run pretty quick, I could throw a smart knife after you." I must have looked quite terrifying as I said this, for B____ dashed away with a scream of horror, downstairs and out of the door.'

When, after B____'s departure, Krespel went to raise Antonia, who was lying senseless on the floor, she opened her eyes with a profound sigh, but seemed to close them again, as if in death. Krespel then broke out into loud, inconsolable lamentations. The doctor, fetched by the old housekeeper, said that Antonia was suffering from a violent shock, but that there was no danger; and this proved to be the case as she recovered even more speedily than was to be expected. She now clung to her father with the most devoted filial affection, and entered warmly into all his favorite hobbies, however absurd. She helped him to take old fiddles to pieces, and to put new ones together. 'I won't sing any more. I want to live for you,' she would often say to him with a gentle smile, when people asked her to sing, and she was obliged to refuse. Krespel endeavored to spare her those trials, and this was why he avoided taking her into society, and tried to taboo all music. He knew, of course, what pain it was to her to renounce the art which she had cultivated to such perfection.

When he bought the remarkable violin already spoken of—the one which was buried with her—and was going to take it to pieces, Antonia looked at him very sorrowfully, and said in gentle imploring tones, 'This one, too?' Some indescribable impulse constrained him to leave it untouched, and to play on it. Scarcely had he brought out a few notes from it when Antonia cried, loudly and joyfully, 'Ah ! that is I—I am singing again.'

And of a verity its silver bell-like tones had something quite extraordinarily wonderful about them. They sounded as if they came out of a human heart. Krespel was deeply affected. He played more gloriously than ever he had done before. And when, with his fullest power, he would go storming over the strings, in brilliant, sparkling scales and arpeggios, Antonia would clap her hands and cry, delighted, 'Ah! I did that well. I did that splendidly!' Often she would say to him, 'I should like to sing something, father'; and then he would take the fiddle from the wall, and play all her favorite songs, those which she used to sing of old—and then she was quite happy.

A short time before I came back, Krespel one night thought he heard someone playing on the piano in the next room, and presently he recognized that it was B____, preluding in his accustomed rather peculiar fashion. He tried to rise from his bed, but some strange heavy weight seemed to lie upon him, fettering him there, so that he could not move. Presently he heard Antonia singing to the piano, in soft whispering tones, which gradually swelled and swelled to the most pealing fortissimo. Then those marvelous tones took the form of a beautiful, glorious aria which B____ had once written for Antonia, in the religious style of the old masters. Krespel said the state in which he found himself was indescribable, for terrible alarm was in it, and also a bliss such as he had never before known. Suddenly he found himself in the middle of a flood of the most brilliant and dazzling light, and in this light he saw B____ and Antonia holding each other closely embraced, and looking at each other in a rapture of bliss. The tones of the singing and of the accompanying piano went on, although Antonia was not seen to be singing, and B____ was not touching the keys. Here Krespel fell into a species of profound unconsciousness, in which the vision and the music faded and were lost. When he recovered, all that remained was a sense of anxiety and alarm.

He hastened into Antonia's room. She was lying on the couch, with her eyes closed, and a heavenly smile on her face, as if she were dreaming of the most exquisite happiness and bliss. But she was dead!

Made in United States
Orlando, FL
21 August 2024